THE PRICE OF SALVATION

A short story

Written by
Denise Tapscott

Edited by Kate Jonez

"Every choice we make requires payment—what would you be willing to pay for redemption? Denise Tapscott's careful pacing reveals, in layers, the price a woman must face for past decisions that should have given her a perfect life."

—Linda D. Addison, award-winning author of "How to Recognize a Demon Has Become Your Friend".

Denise N. Tapscott knocks it out of the ball-park with her refreshing read *The Price of Salvation*! This short tale has horror, humor, and even history - all in the right places. Grandmother Zenobia is my favorite Voodoo High Priestess. She'll be yours, too!

—Blaze McRob, author

"The dark slowly takes hold, like the sun setting over the French Quarter, as a mystery unravels in Denise Tapscott's *The Price of Salvation*. You won't feel the knife go in until it twists!"

—John Palisano, Bram Stoker Award-Winning author of *Ghost Heart*, President of The Horror Writers Association

"If this is your first foray into Denise Tapscott's world, savor every word—it only gets better from here! If you have been eagerly awaiting the new adventures of your favorite characters, you will not be disappointed."

– Tish Booker, author

Denise delivers a short worthy of Tales From The Darkside and Creepshow. It's the kind of cautionary karma story that will frighten you being nicer to people before day's end.

—Steven Van Patten, award winning author of *Killer Genius: She Kills Because She Cares* and *Killer Genius 2: Attack of the Gym Rats*

I was raised in the deep, depressing part of the South; God help me I never wanted to go back there, to those people. Passing skeletal, abandoned homes brought up memories of where I grew up, far away from the glittering lights of Los Angeles, my adopted home and beloved sanctuary. I knew the ride to Carrefour Parish would be arduous.

Having to stop every so often to puke my guts out didn't help either. The trip better be worth it.

After receiving the sweetest kiss I've ever had in my entire life, on my wedding day, everything changed for me. I'd been sick for over two weeks.

First I thought holistic medicine would help. My appointment with my acupuncturist was horrific. The moment she saw my black tongue she screamed at me in Cantonese and kicked me out of her office.

After a barrage of tests at Cedar Sinai in Beverly Hills, while wearing those ridiculous paper gowns, doctors didn't have a clue about what was wrong with me. My husband thought it was all in my head. I love him, but he's an idiot. He's my handsome Prince Charming, but an idiot.

I had my monthly visit with Oceania, "Psychic to the Stars" sporting her turquoise highlights and matching nail polish. She insisted that I travel to New Orleans and see some Hoodoo Voodoo person. Luckily, I thanked her for my "something blue" garter she gave me before I vomited in her turquoise trash can. In between dry heaves and sips of water she offered me, she told me that I'd been cursed, and it was a doozy. Oceania swore the Voodoo High Priestess worked miracles.

The little old lady better be good.

I immediately packed my Louis Vuitton travel bag and told my husband I was going on a trip to review a new boutique in New Orleans. He had no idea what I was really up to.

"Visit my parents. Spend a little time with them in that big old house of theirs," he said. "If we want to stay in their good graces, it would be best if you made an appearance. Besides, you need to return my mother's antique pearl earrings you borrowed for the wedding."

He came from old southern money, and I came from old southern trash. He made a good point, so I couldn't really refuse. His parents hated that I made him escape to California after high school, but he continued to keep the family business successful, so they couldn't argue too loudly.

* * *

It wasn't too long before I found myself standing at the front door of my in-laws mansion. The tall white pillars reminded me of a similar home I visited often as a teenager; a girlfriend I grew up with lived in a smaller mansion, with the same typical hanging gas lamps. Her parents didn't like me very much; she didn't care and neither did I.

George, the family butler greeted me. I'm fairly certain he is almost as old as the house. His knees cracked when escorting me to the parlor where I met up with Mr. and Mrs. Jurel. Although their personalities were lackluster at best, they always wore high end, custom tailored clothing. Mrs. Jurel wore a light tan colored linen dress and her husband wore a button up shirt and matching tan linen slacks. I couldn't tear my eyes away from her freshwater peach pearl earrings with matching pendant and bracelet her husband brought her from his last trip to China. They had enough money to spend on anything they wanted for three lifetimes.

Spending the night in their creaky old mansion was better than I thought. After exchanging pleasantries, we were ushered into the formal dining room where we would be served a five course meal. Sadly, after drinking a glass of filtered water, most of my time was spent on my hands and knees in the guest bathroom. It was decorated with flowers and cherubs, right down to the trash basket next to the toilet.

Once I returned her earrings I borrowed for my wedding, my mother-in-law was unexpectedly polite to me. It was the first time I can remember that we didn't fire off condescending remarks at one another. When they die, it would be unfortunate, but I will have a wonderful time redecorating that huge house. I'd be true southern royalty then.

The next morning I finally arrived in Carrefour Parish. I parked on the side of a dusty, two-lane road, a few feet away from the Voodoo woman's house. I had wanted a shiny silver Rolls Royce, but the rental company only had black, which showed dirt, and scratches. I'd be sure to make a note of their service (or lack thereof) in my article *'The*

Do's and Don'ts of New Orleans'. My work gave new meaning to the old saying "the pen is mightier than the sword." My reviews could make or break any business.

As I managed to shove open the car door, the southern humidity smacked me in the face. Back in Los Angeles, I never dealt with this kind of weather. I was desperate for ocean breezes. This sticky, heavy air was ridiculous. After I managed to stand, my stomach gurgled so loud I swore I scared off a flock of black birds. A nasty, sour belch climbed its way up, escaping through my mouth. At least it wasn't from my ass.

The house seemed miles away. I should have stopped right at the door, but Oceana's instructions were clear. No parking in front of the house.

I trudged along toward the small wooden home. It was actually almost charming, in a southern sort of way. It was odd, though, that it was alone, in the middle of nowhere.

Driving here, I had seen a few shacks and broken down, rusty mobile homes, similar to what I grew up in, and miles and miles of dark green grass. I might have seen an occasional patch of swampland, in between my dry heaves. With the right amount of publicity, I bet I could make New Orleans the newest hot spot around. It's already called Hollywood South.

I was light-headed, but it was probably because I hadn't eaten anything since my honeymoon. I could barely keep down chicken broth. There was a strange buzzing sound in my ears; hopefully it was those pesky June bugs. Without any warning, my stomach balled up like an angry fist. I fell to my knees as bile rushed up through my raw throat. Gravel bit into my knees and the palms of my hands, as I retched hot, sticky fluid. After choking a few times, my stomach relaxed. I was tired of continually grabbing tissue to wipe my face. I was tired of reapplying my favorite lipstick to sore, swollen lips. I was tired of groveling to a porcelain god every day.

I would have given anything to feel normal again.

After backing away from a puddle of frothy bile, I crawled through dry grass, over to a wooden post. I pulled myself up, barely able to stand. I noticed a sparkly ruby red, high-heeled shoe perched on top of the latch of a wooden gate. The instructions said it was a sign that visitors were welcome onto the property. My own, Italian brown leather heels were scuffed and dusty. They'd have to be replaced when I got back home.

Pieces of grass and small bits of gravel were still embedded in my knees. Once I was back to being myself, I would meet with my personal shopper. My clothes didn't fit from all the weight I'd lost. Too bad I wasn't sick before my wedding. Six months ago shedding pounds was almost impossible without a personal trainer. Here I was, not even a month after the ceremony, and my brand new custom made Vera Wang wedding dress fit like a muumuu. The seamstress in the cute bridal shop worked a miracle. Once I got back, I would look her up too.

I glanced at my watch and noticed it was 3 o'clock in the afternoon. Somehow I managed to be on time for my appointment.

Mustering up as much energy as I could, I pressed through the heavy wooden gate. It squeaked, announcing my presence. The vibrant purple front door of the one story home caught my eye.

"That's Tyrian purple," I heard myself say out loud, to no one. The first time I learned about it was in Ancient History class, in the 10th grade. We'd learned random trivia about the Phoenicians. I was popular with lots of people back then too. I don't remember much else I supposedly learned in high school.

I also knew that tidbit from my piece 'Which Museums are Hot or Not'. I discovered an exquisite display of items in London, at an out-of-the-way nautical museum. The purple dye came from snails. The Tyrian color is a symbol of royalty, dating back to the Phoenicians and other ancient civilizations. The Romans couldn't get enough of it. Too bad that little museum was on the "not" list. The drab old curator rambled endlessly. No real food, no adult drinks. Wonderful treasures, but barely even a gift shop. My readers would hate it.

I flirted with the idea of getting a closer look at the color of the Voodoo woman's front door. I was drawn to it. Images of luxury, regalness, crème de la crème opulence flitted through my mind. The instructions I clung to, so fiercely in my sweaty, sticky hand were very clear. DO NOT APPROACH THE FRONT DOOR UNDER ANY CIRCUMSTANCES. As if on cue, another wooden door squeaked from the side of the house.

I glanced up and made a small wish. *Let this be over.*
Large fluffy clouds floated in a blue sky, offering no solace
from the punishing sunlight. Sweat rolled down my back. My
head wouldn't stop pounding. As I drew near wooden stairs
that lead to the side porch, my stomach spasmed. My legs,
too shaky to stand, forced me to crumble, causing 'leakage'
from my butt. I couldn't bear the thought of soiling myself,
again. I cursed as I crawled on achy hands and bruised knees.
I wiped my hair from my face. When I got back to LA, I'd
have my assistant get me an emergency appointment at the
salon. My hair was thin. The blonde highlights needed a
boost too. I missed my witty stylist Michel, the only person
that I could talk to about anything.

Honestly though, I couldn't consider how I looked. I
knew I was hideous. I wanted to curl up in a ball and cry my
eyes out.

I dragged myself through the open doorway and when I entered the humidity vanished. Cool air caressed my face. Somehow I stood up straight and sighed. When was the last time I took an honest deep breath, without coughing or puking? The aroma of freshly baked cinnamon rolls filled the air. My escape from the southern heat was so glorious that I might never leave.

"Settle down," a voice said while my eyes searched in the darkness.

"Close the door, and have a seat, Mrs. Jurel."

The voice of the Voodoo woman was clear and melodic, only slightly tainted with a New Orleans drawl.

After blinking a few times, I saw a small metal folding chair. My eyes still hadn't adjusted to the darkness so I fumbled around until I could sit obediently. The chair was more comfortable than I expected. Resting in the darkness was wonderful. Once I regained my focus, I noticed I was sitting at a small table covered in soft black velvet. I wanted to brush my fingers across it, but my hands were dirty, accented with ragged nails, so I opted instead to fold my hands in my lap.

Sitting on a large purple and gold throne across from me was a pleasant-looking-dark skinned woman. Her hair was covered with a purple turban, matching the royal purple on her front door. She wore a black gauze tunic blouse. Around her neck, a shiny copper Ankh glowed against her skin. She didn't wear any other jewelry, except a large black and gold fleur-de-lis ring that adorned well-manicured fingers. Was she wearing a skirt or pants? I probably shouldn't care what kind of shoes she was wearing, either. She was not the toothless, gray-haired woman I expected. If I were to guess, she looked like she was in her 40s? My assistant Tasha joked "Black don't crack". I could never say that, but I think she's right. This woman didn't look old enough to be a grandmother. She reminded me of that lady with the popular television talk show. Everyone in her studio audience went home with expensive vacations and new cars.

Three fresh, tapered candles, one black, one blue and one white, formed a triangle on the table on my right. A thicker, taller, purple candle sat close to the Voodoo Woman. From my research, I knew the black one warded off negative energies and promoted healing. Royal blue was for seeking wisdom and truth. White was for protection, and purification. Lastly, the purple one was for spiritual protection. All the candles on this table represented protection but the purple one supposedly canceled negative effects of bad karma. The Voodoo woman made interesting choices.

Reluctantly I lifted my head to take in my surroundings. My neck was sore from my head being tossed back and forth every time I vomited. When I glanced around the room, I saw shelves of books, crosses, various kinds of statues and other religious-looking artifacts. If I was not mistaken, there was a shrunken head in the corner. To my left, there was a jade dragon perched on a shiny black surface. Was that a human skull staring down at me? Heavy red velvet curtains with gold trim covered windows, presumably protecting us from the sun. In another corner there were large, dusty trunks. Simply being in this spooky room was worth my $500 dollars.

"Mrs. Jurel, you look like you could use some water."

Grandmother Zenobia handed me a chilled, plastic bottle of water. I was scared to drink it; when I vomited all over the luxurious black velvet table, I would be mortified.

"Go on, drink."

I swirled the cool water in my mouth a few times before swallowing. I braced for the burn. Instead the liquid was sweet and went down smoothly. It was an ordinary bottle of water, but it felt like I was drinking tears from heaven. I paused, waiting for my stomach to betray me. It rumbled for a moment but then, silence. Carelessly, I chugged the water as fast as I could. Panicked, I look around for a trash can, for when my body-double crossed me and the water forced its way back out.

There was no trash can. There was no vomit. There was peace, while sitting in a cool room. I was so grateful that I cried.

"Do you need a moment to collect yourself?" She asked, while passing me a tissue. It was softer than the ones I've religiously kept at my side. Wiping my tears away, I noticed my eyes didn't sting when I blinked. I cried even more. It would take centuries to stop sobbing and catch my breath.

Attempting to compose myself, I noticed that I sat taller. My fever faded away. "Thank you, Zenobia."

"Feeling better?" she asked.

"Yes," I can't believe that I actually *do* feel better. Thank you so much for seeing me."

"I prefer to be called Grandmother Zenobia."

The black candle, the one for healing, flared brighter than the others, illuminating the room. The voodoo woman mumbled to herself; the flame obeyed her muttered commands and returned to its regular state.

I re-adjusted in my seat and for the first time in months, I was almost my old self. I took in another deep breath and appreciated the smell of cinnamon again. Aware I was on the clock, I got down to business.

"You know, you should change your name. You'd get more customers and followers, if you were on social media. You don't look old enough to be a Grandmother. Try something like 'Lady Z' or 'Madame Zenobia'. Those names are easier to sell. It's about your brand, know what I mean?" Words poured from my lips faster than I guzzled the water.

The Voodoo woman stared at me, with one eyebrow raised. The floor board behind me creaked like a cue for me to stop rambling.

"Apologies. I always look for business opportunities for people."

The pesky black candle sparked a few times and then continued to shine with the others.

Grandmother broke her cold stare. She looked to my right for a moment and then shrugged.

"It's your session. We can chat about whatever you like."

She pulled out a worn deck of tarot cards and shuffled. The edges were black, slightly curled. The deck was Ivory colored and had black swirls, with tiny roses.

"As you saw when I first came in, I'm not well. I haven't been able to eat or drink anything for a while. A psychic back in Los Angeles sent me."

"Ah yes, Oceania. She's sweet."

"She is, but eccentric with the crazy hair and nails, don't you think? Anyways, I did my research. You are a bona fide Voodoo High Priestess, highly recommended by her and a few others."

She nodded, as if I were chatting about the weather. She seemed too casual and I needed her to know I meant business.

"Before we continue Zenobia I'm laying a few ground rules. First, I ask most of the questions, not you.

Second, I expect you to keep my dealings private. If I choose to let people know I was here, it's because I decide, not you. If all goes well, I could make it possible for you to have a line of people waiting outside your door. Third, if you shake a rattle at me and then make a snake burst through an egg, I will walk right out of that door and demand my money back. I refuse to pay for parlor tricks. For what it's worth, I like the candles. They're a nice touch."

The Voodoo woman smiled to herself and continued to shuffle the cards.

All three candles close to me flickered. The purple one was undisturbed.

"Settle down." she said.

"Excuse me?"

"Is there anything else, Mrs. Jurel?" she asked as she studied my face.

"No, I guess that's about it, Lady Z." I'm not sure why, but I had a hard time looking directly at her.

"How about we start with a general reading from the Tarot cards?"

"No. Do a seven card spread. I want details."

"Sure thing."

She set the deck before me. I noticed it was cooler in the room than before. I didn't mind it too much, but if it continued I would ask for a window to be cracked open or the A/C to be turned down.

"Shuffle the cards for as long as you'd like. Clear your thoughts and when you are ready, create three, smaller separate stacks."

The cards were soft. As I shuffled, I swore I smelled roses. I looked closely at the back of one card to examine the details. It was just paper, with little black lines and drawings of red roses. It was a weird trick, but I liked it.

The obvious question I wanted to ask was, "why was this happening to me?" It was always so hard to clear your mind when someone told you to do it. I took stupid yoga classes. At the end, you lie around and focus on breathing. "Sink into the earth" the vegan tree-hugging yogi said. I only went because they were the latest craze around town. Clear my mind? Yeah right.

I needed to get on with this. I growled and made three small stacks.

Lady Z (as I've decided to call her) collected the cards, then methodically placed a total of seven cards before me, face up. As each card was revealed, she studied them and nodded her head.

The feisty black candle, the one for negative energies and healing, sputtered and extinguished by itself.

"Are you going to re-light that one?"

"No, that's not how it works."

"I see. All right then Lady Z, go for it."

"The first card is the Princess of Swords. Some call it the Page of Swords. This card is reversed. It represents a woman in your life, or a feminine energy. She is jealous and represents a difficult lesson you need to learn."

The folding chair I was sitting on wasn't as comfortable as when I first sat down.

"The second card is the Wheel of Fortune. It represents the universe as it spins its wheel over people's lives. If you pass tests placed before you by God, good things will come to you."

So far, I was not enjoying this reading.

Lady Z continued to go over the cards. There was the reversed Hanged Man, Death, the Tower, and the Page of

Cups, reversed. The last card was the reversed Empress.

The cards all looked and sounded miserable. She rambled on and on about lessons to be learned, transformation, blah blah blah. The reversed Empress represented a blockage of feminine energy, the loss of a loved one and something about vanity.

None of this was new. When Oceania did my reading, she insisted that the reversed Empress card represented my mother. My mother was dead to me, literally and figuratively. Before she died, she begged for me to come home to the trailer park and help out with the family. Going back there would never be an option for me. It was her fault she and the Catholic Church didn't believe in birth control. It was her fault that half of her 13 kids came out retarded. She told me she had a chance, once, to leave my father. She stayed for my sake. For my sake? I didn't ask her to make that sacrifice for me. She was too stupid to get government assistance. She always said the family had "too much honor.

Welfare was for colored folk". It was her fault they were poor white trash and stayed white trash. I was lucky to escape when I did.

I realized that I was lost in thought while Zenobia went on with my reading.

"Zee, where did you get that turban? Is it a scarf? I simply must have one like it." It was rude to interrupt someone but I didn't care. I pretended that I was bored but actually I was scared shitless. I didn't like where this reading was going.

She stopped and shook her head. "I've had this thing for so long I honestly don't remember."

"I noticed it's the same color as your front door, and the candle on your left. That's a hard color to get, if it's the real deal. Not that you would have real Tyrian purple paint or dye. The dye is from snails. It goes back to…"

"Mrs. Jurel, let me stop you."

I put on my best poker face for whatever it was she was going to say. If this was about my mother, I was running out the door.

"The overall picture is that you have a communication problem."

"I have a communication problem?" I thought she'd go a different way. "I'm a great communicator. Have you read any of my magazine articles? They're everywhere. I have thousands of fans and followers on social media. Did you see my wedding announcement in the New York Times? It's impossible to get a spot, but we did."

Surely this woman had heard of me, even if I hadn't heard of her. People loved me.

"The problem is that you talk too much and most of it is deceptive. You manipulate people and their words."

"Are you calling me a liar?" Clearly she was going on my 'not list' of New Orleans.

The Voodoo woman mumbled something and collected the tarot cards.

The royal blue candle, the one for wisdom and truth, did the same flicker trick as the black one. It sparked a few times and kept shining.

"Why are you here, really?" she asked me point-blank. "I know that this was the exact same spread you've received from Oceania and a handful of other spiritual people. If you don't want the truth, then say so. We can sit and be social. You have some time left in your session."

A cold chill ran down my spine. There were no open windows. There was no fan. Yet a cold breeze passed right by me. How does she know that it's the exact same spread? The information was supposed to be private. The pictures of the cards from other readings looked different, but she was right. I knew it was the exact same spread, again. I couldn't escape it.

"Girlfriend, I'll be honest. I'm here because someone cursed me. I need to know who did it, and why."

"Why didn't you say so, instead of wasting my time? That's easy."

Why did I test this woman? If she had the answer I need, I could be rid of the curse and get back to being me. Maybe I could help her get more business or whatever it is she wanted. She was back on my 'do list.'

"Rhoda Jurel, *I* am the one who cursed you."

The blue candle glowed. Its flame changed from yellow to dark green, to blue.

I practically fell out of my seat.

"YOU CURSED ME?"

"Settle down." she said simply.

"Oh, no. How dare you tell me to settle down!"

The flame of blue candle exploded, leaving only the white candle active on my side of the table. It was the most important anyway, representing protection and purification. It was strange that the purple one still burned steadily.

I stood up, knocking the chair away. I looked for something I could use to hurt this woman. Something snatched the back of my head and scratched my scalp. What kind of trick was this?

"I wasn't talking to you, Mrs. Jurel," the Voodoo woman said. She looked to my right and waved her hand dismissively.

"Pick up the chair and have a seat." She pointed at me, indicating that now she *was* talking to me.

I realized that I hadn't vomited in the past half hour. I was weak and smelly, but I was all right. Or at least I *was*. We were alone, but I had that creepy feeling someone was watching when no one was there. I didn't want to sit, but if I left, I might never know what it was like to feel normal again. I had to be rid of the curse once and for all. Like a child following orders, I picked up the folding chair and returned to my place at the table.

"Why are you doing this to me?" My words weren't clipped and polished. My stupid southern twang wormed its way back into my life. How was that possible? I paid good money for diction classes.

"Sally Mae Ramelle," she said, like it had a grandiose meaning.

"What in the hell does…"

No matter how hard I tried, the drawl was still there.

"Watch your language in my presence," warned the Voodoo woman.

The black velvet card table rattled.

"You're safe." she said, looking over my head. I turned around and saw nothing but a small sliver of light coming from the door I came in.

"She died because of you."

The table stopped shaking.

"I hardly think…"

"That is another problem, for another day."

"What?"

The Voodoo woman kept talking, not skipping a beat.

"Sally Mae tells me you are a bully. The way you run your mouth, I see it's true."

The room was freezing. My teeth chattered. I wished I could stand in the Southern sun, to warm up.

The white candle for healing and purification burned boldly. Smoke slowly swirled over the flame. Then the name clicked for me.

"What do you mean, Sally Mae told ya?"

"Now's your chance. Take your time, like we discussed," said Grandmother Zenobia. She was not looking at me while she spoke. It appeared she was having a conversation with someone else.

"I understand," she said.

She turned her full attention back to me.

"Sally Mae wants an apology. She says you used to be best friends. Her parents didn't like you, but she didn't care."

Little Sally Mae. That bitch. She had the same beautiful, thick straight hair as my ma. I've spent a fortune at the salon to wrangle my hair.

"The day she told you that she lost her virginity to Cedric Jurel, you decided you hated her."

Hot wax dripping from the white candle, turned blood red, as it ran down the sides into the candle holder. I ain't never seen nothing like it.

"What in the hell kind of trick candle is that?"

"Language! This candle is for Sally's protection, and your purification. It's melting red wax because red stimulates personal power. Sally is regaining courage and her power to stand up to her enemy."

"My purification?"

"This is your last chance to come clean. You humiliated that girl in front of other people whenever you had a chance. You insisted that everyone hated her. You tormented her for quite some time. I've seen the letters you thought were destroyed. The bible says "Thou shall not bear false witness, Exodus 20:16."

I wanted the Voodoo woman to shut her ugly mouth, but I couldn't stop her.

"Obviously Sally gave up. She was too weak to fight against your intimidation. The rest is history. Personally, I suspect she reminds you of your mother. I had a nice chat with her too. You didn't get along with her either. By the way, don't bother returning her old pin you wore at your wedding."

Grandmother winked at something near me.

"Sally Mae's spirit was awakened the day you married her boyfriend Cedric. You were wed on the anniversary of her death, not that you paid any mind to that. Sally's distraught mother asked for my assistance. After talking to her, talking to *your* mother --may she now rest in peace--and Sally, I agreed to hex you. The request was justified. Something old, something new, something borrowed, something blue did the trick."

I could only sit, speechless at the stupid table. Sally was really here? That was impossible. Yet, no one knew what I did to her. She was the teacher's pet in every class we had together. Always Miss Goodie Two Shoes, so pretty and so smart. Everyone liked her. When we were supposed to graduate high school, she could go anywhere she wanted, be whoever she wanted to be with perfect, rich Cedric. I couldn't stand her. She had to die.

Another chill passed by me. The white candle flared six inches high and I swear I saw a shadow to my right.

"I cursed you because you hurt Sally and other people around you. You are jealous and insecure. You make others feel worse, to feel better yourself.

"You win, Zee. What now?

"My name is Grandmother Zenobia," she corrected me. "To remove my curse, you must pay me $500,000 by sundown tomorrow, and say a prayer of forgiveness with Sally. I accept cash, cashier's check, or wire transfer to this account." She slid a white piece of paper with a bank account number across the black velvet table over to me. "I'm sure you can understand why I don't take personal checks over $500."

"$500,000 and a prayer?"

"Sally wants me to charge you an additional $25,000 for adultery, but she never married Cedric. He's such a nice man. Anyways, I'm going off track. You can try to get someone else to lift my curse. Won't work. If Papa Lou and the Broken Army catch wind of you, you'll be in far worse trouble than you were when you came through my door.

Psychics and shamans say the curse is karma. Fortune tellers will laugh at you. Santeria specialist and Wicca people won't touch you with a ten-foot pole. Neither the neighborhood Catholic priest down the street, nor your fancy pastor in that mega church in Los Angeles will bother sniffing in my direction. We spiritual people have a large, tight knit community."

The Voodoo woman pulled out a gold pocket watch.

"If it matters at all to you, and it probably doesn't, the money goes to good causes. Aside from my personal fee, some of the funds will go to Sally's family. They've suffered a lot. The rest will go to the National Suicide Prevention Lifeline, a few groups that fight against bullying in schools, and programs to assist and educate people fighting depression."

"If I don't pay and pray?"

"As soon as you walk out that door, the curse will return. You'll be dead in three days. Maybe sooner, judging by how you crawled your way here in the first place. Sally Mae says she's excited to escort you to hell herself."

A cold, gray mist shimmered right next to me. I rubbed my eyes in disbelief. Sally Mae Ramelle stood before me. Her face was pale, her eyes dark as the black stones found in my koi pond. Dark red tracks ran down her arms where she slit them lengthwise with a razor. Her lips were blue from all the pills she swallowed. She was damp head to toe from the bath she died in. She followed my suicide instructions perfectly.

The white candle sparked a few times and died. My stomach quivered and spasmed.

The ghost of Sally Mae rushed at me, howling in my face. I closed my eyes but her screams blasted in my ears. Hot scratches burned my face.

I should have been lounging at a spa, not cowering in a prayer room. My husband would have me committed if I told him I needed $500,000. Or worse, my wicked, old-money mother-in-law would insist he file for divorce. Their pack of lawyers would make sure I didn't have a cent to my name. I couldn't have that. I'd rather die than be poor again.

"Your time is up," said Grandmother Zenobia as she blew out her purple Karma candle. I bet she had the audacity to smile at me in the darkness.

I could barely hear her voice over Sally's screaming...

Denise was born and raised in California. She left her heart in San Francisco, but somehow managed to leave her soul in New Orleans. When she's not creating and cultivating her characters, she enjoys dining on spicy tuna rolls, sharing a bottle of red wine with friends and watching the latest flick (especially scary films). From time to time this radiant left-handed pirate will even challenge others to a fencing match or two. But, watch out. This Gemini is determined to win!

Often referencing her favorite quotes, below is Denise's favorite motto by Hans Christian Andersen:

"Just living is not enough...one must have sunshine, freedom and a little flower."

Denise can be found on twitter @DeniseNTapscott

and Instagram @pyratesunny and more

information/recommendations/updates can also be found on

www.denisetapscott.com

www.ingramcontent.com/pod-product-compliance
Lightning Source LLC
Chambersburg PA
CBHW020321150626
46552CB00022B/3085